OUR GOOSE

(Based on a true story)

Lynn Woollacott

Illustrated by Bugsy

Three geese wriggle in a sack. It's dark inside,

the geese have a long bumpy ride.

Released in a barn in the middle of the night,

a farm horse neighs with fright.

Our Goose thinks the horse is so sweet he deserves a treat.

'Beware of Fox, he's outside in his smart red coat!'

Monday the horse warns.

'Let's make a din and scare Fox away.'

And together, they did.

In the morning three geese shiver by the barn.

The fields are white with snow on the farm. Walter-Jack carries a sack!

Monday stamps his hooves, the geese try to flee

but Goose number two and three can't get free.

They honk inside Walter-Jack's sack, 'We will come back'.

Locked in the barn, Monday neighs,

'They've gone for the farmer's dinner!

'I'll set you free Our Goose!'

He kicks the barn doors until they are loose.

Trudging through snow fields all alone,

Our Goose tries to fly to the geese in the sky

but he can't fly. He begins to cry.

'Your wings are clipped,' says a kind deer,

'Stay the night with us amongst the trees.'

'Fox can't get in, with our antlers, we'll make a din.'

And so, they did. (*Can you spot Our Goose?*)

'It's morning, Our Goose, and time for us to say good-bye.

You should be safe on the pond,' said the deer.

But wait – an hour goes by, what's all that noise in the sky?

Back in the barn, the scent of leather saddle,
but no goose's waddle. Cissie says,
'Let's follow the tracks in the snow,
they might lead us where we need to go.'

Our Goose is found. Lifted on Monday's back, he warms up in a sack.

Soon it is spring, Our Goose is pecking in the farmyard,

WHEN

B RRRRRRR!

B RRRRRRR!

B RRRRRRR!

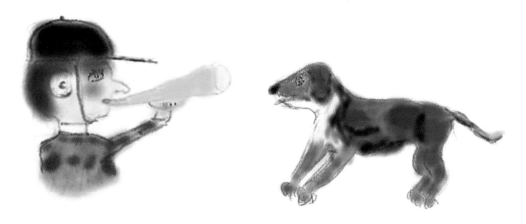

'**TALLY HO!**' cries a huntsman.

'**BARK, BARK**' bellow fifty hounds.

CLOP CLOP tread a hundred horses' hooves.

'**NEIGH!**' cries Monday, '**Our Goose, get high up in the barn!**'

And Our Goose ran to the barn. The hay was trembling,
something was rumbling and it had a black nose and two pointy ears…

Our Goose pulls up hay to cover Fox's ears,
and then sits on Fox's hay covered back.

Outside in the yard, a huntsman on horseback cries, 'Have you seen Fox!?'

'Neigh. Not I,' whinnied Monday.

'He's not here,' shouted Walter-Jack, rattling a sack.

Our Goose tells Fox to stay hidden until dark

and then he goes to the kitchen to beg for scraps to feed to Fox.

Finally, Fox's tummy stops rumbling.

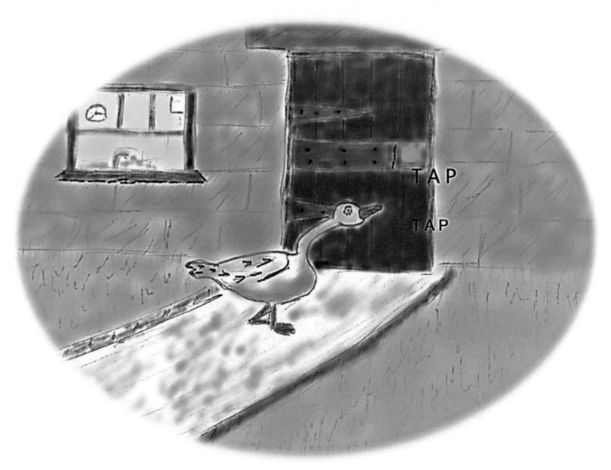

Soon Easter arrives. Our Goose is captured in a sack!

'**No! No!** We'll have none of that!' cries Cissie to Walter-Jack.

In the farmyard she lets Our Goose loose.

Our Goose keeps cool
in an old tin bath.

Cissie comes to show Our Goose her baby in her own cradle.

As baby Celia grows, she feeds Our Goose,

takes him little walks

and shows him picture books in the kitchen.

A few days later, Walter-Jack brings home seven white geese.

They waddle and gaggle.

'Hello,' says Our Goose. 'Shall I show you around the farm?'

And he did.

Soon after that Our Goose shows Cissie his creamy-white egg.

The egg is cold, the shell won't crack and there's no *cheep cheeps.*

'Oh, Our Goose, all this time you were a **GIRL** goose. You can't have goslings of your own.'

Outside a mother goose's goslings are on their way to the pond,

'Cheep cheep cheep,' calls a stray.

Our Goose hears him, runs, and gathers him under her wings.

The goslings cheer for **'Auntie Goose,'** and the other mums ask for her help

with all the goslings.

Fox comes in the night, gives the geese a terrible fright,

he drops something small and squirmy, by the barn.

'MEOW,' cries a kitten.

Our Goose calls him inside, where he stays by her side.

They call the kitten, Friday.

The next winter two geese fly down from the sky.

'OUR GOOSE SISTER,' they cry with joy.

'You know you can fly again? Your clipped wing feathers have grown back.'

Her brothers told her Walter-Jack had taken them to market to exchange for

seeds. Their wings feathers had grown back, and they had flown away, and

found a new pond to live by, they had been searching ever since for Our Goose.

With promise of visits from their quite far-away pond,

Our Goose decides to stay, to snuggle down at night with her best friends in the hay.

For Grace, Jacob, Ethan, Daniel and Pixie.

My special thanks to Celia Hawkins, Bugsy and Tree.

Celia recounts her memories of 'Philis'.

I was born mid-WW2, in 1943, food was rationed, and country people used their initiative to become as self-sufficient as possible. My parents Walter and Cissie Rumsey were given three geese. By Easter my mother had grown fond of goose number one. My mother said, 'No more of that!' My mother named him Philip until one day he laid an egg (her eggs never hatched) his name was promptly changed to Philis.

Philis' was a greylag goose. We acquired another seven white geese. Over the years the goslings were regularly sold at Wymondham Market, Norfolk, the money raised put towards holidays.

Philis like to wrap her long neck around mine and I'd place my arms around her. We often spent time together like this. Our friendship grew and formed a large part of my growing up in a happy, caring environment with the cat, Friday, Philis and the other geese …

Jack at Christmas, by Daniel, Age 10

First Edition: **OUR GOOSE**

Printed in Great Britain
by Amazon

84782869R00016